A Very Crazy Christmas

#1: Tooth Trouble
#2: The King of Show-and-Tell
#3: Homework Hassles
#4: Don't Sit on My Lunch!
#5: Talent Show Scaredy-Pants
#6: Help! A Vampire's Coming!
#7: Yikes! Bikes!
#8: Halloween Fraidy-Cat
#9: Shark Tooth Tale
#10: Super-Secret Valentine
#11: The Pumpkin Elf Mystery
#12: Stop That Hamster!
#13: The One Hundredth Day of School!
#14: Camping Catastrophe!
#15: Thanksgiving Turkey Trouble
#16: Ready, Set, Snow!
#17: Firehouse Fun!
#18: The Perfect Present
#19: The Penguin Problem
#20: Apple Orchard Race
#21: Going Batty
#22: Science Fair Flop
#23: A Very Crazy Christmas

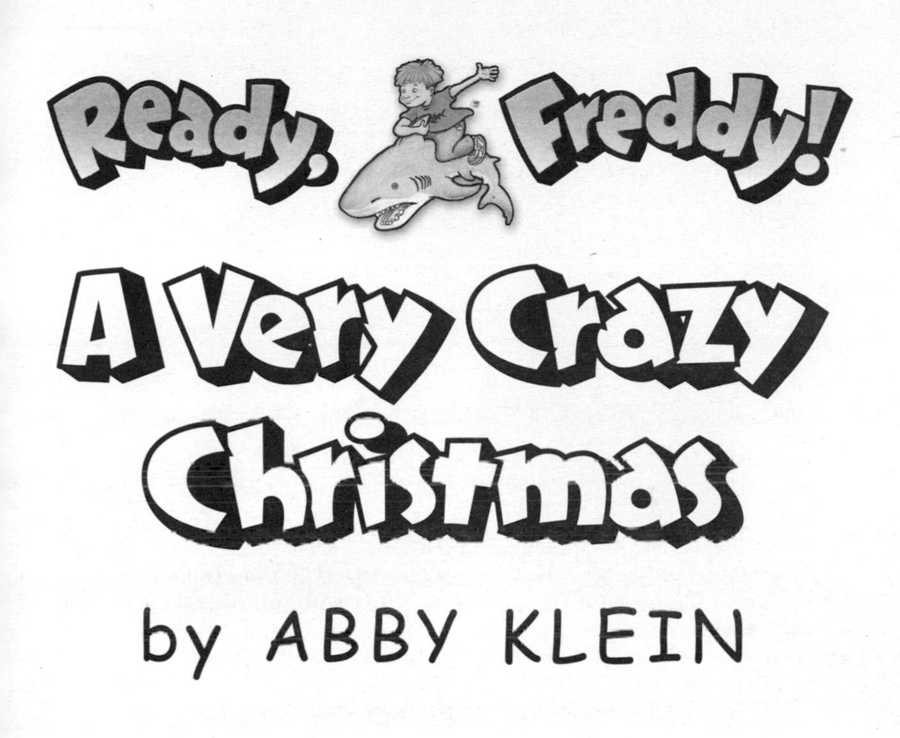

by ABBY KLEIN

illustrated by
JOHN McKINLEY

Scholastic Inc.
New York Toronto London Auckland
Sydney Mexico City New Delhi Hong Kong

To Harry, Shirley, Michael, Susan, Amy, Rich, Sue, Niki, Ashley, Joel, Josh, and Dani. Being with you makes every Christmas special!

I love you all!
—A.K.

ISBN 978-0-545-29497-3

12 11 10 9 8 7 6 11 12 13 14 15 16/0

Printed in the U.S.A. 40
First printing, September 2011

CHAPTERS

I have a problem.

A really, really big problem.

My twin cousins, Kelly and Kasey,

are coming for Christmas,

and whenever they're around,

things get a little crazy!

Let me tell you about it.

CHAPTER 1

Happy Holidays

"Have a great holiday, everyone!" said our teacher, Mrs. Wushy, as we ran out the door.

I raced out of school, jumped on the bus, and plopped down in my seat. My best friend Robbie sat down next to me.

"This is going to be the best Christmas ever!" I said to Robbie.

"Why?" Max butted in. "Are you going to dance in *The Nutcracker* ballet?" Then Max stood up and announced to the whole bus,

"Guess what, everybody? Freddy is going to wear a tutu and dance in *The Nutcracker*!"

The whole bus started laughing, and my face got hot. I sank down in my seat.

"Really?" said Chloe. "I'm going to wear a tutu and dance in *The Nutcracker*. What color is your tutu, Freddy?"

"Yeah, what color is your tutu, Freddy?" Max said, imitating Chloe.

I sank lower in my seat. "I wish I could disappear," I whispered to Robbie.

Just then my other best friend, Jessie, looked right at Max and said, "What color is *your* tutu, Max?"

For a minute Max couldn't say anything. Then he stammered, "I-I-I don't have a tutu."

"Yes, you do," said Jessie. "It's pink and has sparkles on it."

The whole bus burst out laughing. Max's cheeks got red, and he quickly sat down in his seat.

“Thanks, Jessie,” I said. Jessie was so brave. She was the only one brave enough to stand up to Max, the biggest bully in the whole first grade.

“No problem,” said Jessie, giggling.

"What's so funny?" I asked.

"Nothing," said Jessie. "I'm just thinking of Max in a sparkly pink tutu. I bet he looks just like a little princess when he wears it."

Robbie, Jessie, and I started laughing so hard I thought we were going to fall out of our seats.

"So, Freddy," said Robbie. "You still haven't told us why this is going to be the best Christmas ever."

I smiled a big, wide smile. "Kelly and Kasey are coming to visit," I said.

"Who?" asked Jessie.

"My twin cousins, Kelly and Kasey. Papa Dave and Grammy Rose are coming, and they're bringing the twins with them."

"Why are they coming with your grand-parents?" Robbie asked.

"Well, their whole family was supposed to come, but my baby cousin Kenny got the chicken pox, so my aunt and uncle have to stay home with him," I said.

"At least *they* still get to come," said Robbie.

"Are they older or younger than you?" asked Jessie.

"They're older than me, but not as old as Suzie," I said.

"You sound so excited," said Jessie.

"I can't wait! Things always get a little crazy when those two are around."

"My Christmas is going to be extra special, too," said Jessie. "My *abuela*, my grandma, says that this year I'm old enough to carry my own candle for *Las Posadas*."

"Las Po-what?" I said.

"Las Posadas," said Jessie. "It's a Mexican Christmas celebration. Everybody lights candles and then walks through the streets. It's kind of like a parade."

"Cool," I said. "That sounds really beautiful."

"It is," said Jessie. "It's always my favorite part of Christmas."

"How about you?" I asked Robbie. "Do you get to do anything special this year?"

"Yes! My mom says I can light the kinara this year."

"The what?" I asked.

"The kinara."

"I've never heard of that," said Jessie.

"Well, my family doesn't celebrate

Christmas," said Robbie. "We celebrate Kwanzaa. The kinara is a candleholder that holds seven candles. We light one each night to celebrate the harvest."

"That sounds like the menorah that my family lights for Hanukkah," said Max.

I didn't even know he was listening to us.

"It is a lot like a menorah," said Robbie.

"Do you want to know what my favorite part of Hanukkah is?" asked Max.

"Not really," I whispered to Robbie. "It's when my mom makes potato pancakes."

"That sounds disgusting," said Chloe, wrinkling up her nose. "Who makes pancakes out of potatoes?"

"For your information, little prissy princess," said Max, "they are delicious!"

"That does sound good," said Jessie. "It sounds like a giant hash brown."

"That's exactly what they're like, and they taste really good with applesauce," Max said, licking his lips.

"You know, Chloe," said Jessie, "you really shouldn't say something sounds disgusting if you've never tried it."

"Yeah," said Max.

"Hmph," Chloe said as she tossed her strawberry-blonde curls and turned away.

"My favorite Christmas food is gingerbread cookies," I said, patting my stomach.

"I love those, too!" said Max.

"I like putting all the colored sprinkles on them," I said.

"Yeah. That's my favorite part, too!" said Max.

"Wow! Something we have in common," I whispered to Robbie.

I smiled at Max.

I think he might have actually smiled back at me.

Just then the bus pulled up in front of my house.

I jumped out of my seat. "Good-bye, everybody," I called. "Happy holidays!"

"Good-bye, Freddy," said Robbie. "Hope you have a great Christmas!"

"Oh, I will! This is going to be a very crazy Christmas!"

CHAPTER 2

Jingle All the Way

That night at dinner I was so excited I was bouncing in my seat.

"Freddy, please calm down," said my mom. "You are going to fall out of your chair."

"I can't sit still, Mom. I am so excited about Christmas! This is going to be the best Christmas ever!" I started to sway and sing, "Jingle bells, jingle bells, jingle all the way."

"It's going to be the *worst* Christmas ever

if you keep singing," said my sister, Suzie, covering her ears.

"Suzie, that's not very nice to say to your brother," said my dad.

"Well, he sounds like a sick goat in the manger," Suzie said, laughing.

I didn't care what she said tonight. I was in too good a mood. I just kept singing and swaying. "Jingle bells, jingle bells."

"Freddy smells," Suzie sang.

I ignored her and sang louder. "JINGLE ALL THE WAY!" But this time I swayed a little too far to one side and fell right off my chair.

"Ha, ha, ha!" Suzie laughed. "That was a good one, Freddy!"

My mom jumped out of her chair and ran over to me. "Freddy, Freddy, are you all right?"

I looked up at her from my spot on the floor, and then I popped up, ran over to Suzie, and sang in her ear, "Jingle bells, Suzie smells."

Suzie stuck her tongue out at me.

"That's enough, you two," said my dad. "This is the holidays. A time for peace and love. Freddy, go back to your seat."

"Papa and Grammy and your cousins are coming any minute," said my mom.

"Really?" I said. "I can't wait!"

"Tomorrow we are going to take Kelly and Kasey with us to get a Christmas tree," said my mom.

"At White's Tree Farm," I interrupted. "We get to chop down our own tree. Right, Dad?" I jumped out of my chair and pretended to swing an ax. "Hi-ya!"

"That's right," my dad said, laughing. "But we are not ninja woodcutters. We will be using a little saw."

"I can do that!" I said, sawing at the air.

"Hey, Shark Breath, we are not playing charades," said Suzie. "Sit down and let Mom finish."

"Sorry, Mom. I'm just so excited!" I sat back down.

"I think I've almost got all of the presents wrapped," said my mom. "We had so many extra presents to wrap this year."

"Really?" I said. "Extra presents!" I leaned across the table. "Did you hear that, Suzie? We get extra presents this year! This really is going to be the best Christmas ever!"

"I didn't say *you* get extra presents," said my mom.

"Oh," I mumbled.

"Yeah, Ding-Dong," said Suzie. "The extra presents are for our guests. Right, Mom?"

"You mean Papa and Grammy and the twins?" I asked.

"No, the Easter Bunny," said Suzie.

"I didn't know that the Easter Bunny got Christmas presents."

"Freddy, are you for real? Of course she

means Papa and Grammy and the twins!" said Suzie.

"I just know Kelly and Kasey are going to love the present I picked out for them," I said.

"The present *you* picked out?" said Suzie. "*I* was the one who picked it out."

"No, I did!"

"I did!"

I skipped right over to her chair, bent down, and whispered in her ear, "I did."

Suzie jumped up and started chasing me around the table like we were playing duck duck goose.

As we were running, my dad stuck out his arms and grabbed us. We both froze. "Listen, you two. We have a lot to do before Christmas. If you can't behave, maybe we'll just have to cancel Christmas."

I stared at him. "Did you just say 'cancel Christmas'?"

"Yes, I did."

"You can't cancel Christmas! Our cousins are coming, and what about Santa? You can't just cancel Santa!"

"Well, then, I think you should both sit down and listen to your mother."

We ran back to our seats and sat down.

"You both helped pick out the present, and I'm sure your cousins are going to love it," my mom said.

"I know something else we have to do, Mom," said Suzie. "The cookies!"

"Mmmmm, gingerbread cookies," I said, licking my lips.

"Of course we have to make gingerbread cookies," said my mom. "It's a Thresher family tradition."

"I can taste them already," said my dad.

"Me, too!" I said.

"It wouldn't be Christmas without homemade gingerbread cookies," said my mom.

"Did you get the rainbow sprinkles?" asked Suzie.

"How about the little candy buttons?"

"And the raisins for eyes?"

"I got it all," my mom said, laughing. "I thought it would be fun to bake the cookies when Grammy and your cousins were here."

We heard the crunch of tires on snow. Then a car door slammed.

"Shh, I think they're here," said my dad.

"Woohoo!" I said, and pumped my fist in the air.

The doorbell rang.

"They're here! They're here!" Suzie shouted, and she went running toward the door.

I raced after her, smiling. "Now things are going to get a little bit crazy," I said.

CHAPTER 3

They're Here!

Suzie threw open the front door, and Kelly and Kasey burst into the house. "Merry Christmas, everyone!" they shouted.

They grabbed Suzie's hands, and the three of them started jumping up and down and squealing.

"Where's Freddy?" asked Kasey.

"Here I am!" I yelled, and before I could even say hello, they both ran over and tackled me to the ground. "Merry Christmas, Freddy Spaghetti!" they said.

"We are so glad you girls are here!" my mom said.

"Thanks for inviting us, Aunt Debbie," they said.

"Hey, where are Papa and Grammy?" I asked.

"Here we are!" they said. "We were just grabbing some things out of the car."

I ran over to them and gave them a great big hug. "I am so glad you are both here!" I said. "I love it when you come for Christmas!"

"And we love being with all of you," said Grammy Rose.

"And this Christmas will be extra special, because we brought your cousins along," said Papa Dave.

"Bringing Kelly and Kasey is the best Christmas present ever!" said Suzie. The three girls all started squealing again.

"Boy, am I glad I only have one daughter," my dad said, laughing.

"Let's put everybody's things away, and then we can all have some hot chocolate," said my mom. "Freddy, would you please help Papa and Grammy take their things up to your room?"

My room? I didn't know they were staying in there. "Where am I sleeping?" I asked.

"In Suzie's room with your cousins. I thought that might be fun."

"Yeah!" said Kelly and Kasey. "It will be like a big slumber party!"

"Me and three girls. That should be interesting!" I thought.

"Come on, guys, follow me," said Suzie. "I'll help you put your stuff in my room."

"Give me that bag, Papa," I said. "I'll carry it up for you."

"This bag is really heavy," said Papa Dave. "Maybe I should carry that one."

"Nope. I've got it, Papa," I said as I grabbed

the suitcase and started dragging it up the stairs. I didn't want to look like a wimp in front of my cousins.

"Wow! You're strong!" said Kelly.

"Like Superman!" said Kasey.

I smiled.

When they had all put their suitcases away, we went down to the kitchen to drink the hot chocolate.

"Here you go, girls," my mom said to the twins as she handed them each a mug.

They both just stared at their cups.

"Is there something wrong?"

"It's just that we're used to drinking hot chocolate with whipped cream and marshmallows," said Kasey.

"No problem. Coming right up!" said my mom. "All you have to do is ask."

"All you have to do is ask?" I thought. Whenever I ask, I'm usually allowed to have only one or the other!

"Freddy, would you please get the whipped cream out of the refrigerator while I get the marshmallows?"

"Sure thing, Mom," I said, licking my lips.

I grabbed the can and handed it to Kasey. "Here you go," I said. "Whipped cream is one of my favorite things in the whole world."

"Mine, too!" said Kasey.

The next thing I knew, Kasey popped the top and started spraying the whipped cream on my chin.

Just then my mom came back to the table with the marshmallows and saw the whipped cream on my face. "Freddy! What are you doing?" yelled my mom. "That is supposed to go in your hot chocolate, not on your face!"

I tried to say, "Kasey did it," but my mouth was covered in whipped cream.

"Look, it's Santa!" said Kelly, pointing at me.

"Ho, ho, ho," I said. "I'm Santa Claus." I

turned to Suzie. “Have you been a good little girl?”

Kelly and Kasey started giggling, and then Suzie joined in. Pretty soon everyone at the table started laughing.

Usually I get in big trouble when I play with

my food, but this time all my mom could do was laugh. "Oh, Freddy, you are so silly," she said.

I stuck out my tongue and started to lick the whipped cream off my face. "Ooooh, yummy!" I said.

"Freddy!" said my mom. "Let me wipe that off your face, and then you can put some in your hot chocolate."

My mom cleaned me up, and I squirted whipped cream into my cup.

I started to drink, but Kasey grabbed my arm. "Wait, wait, wait! You forgot something," she said.

"I did?"

"Yep. Marshmallows." She grabbed a handful and threw them up in the air. "Look! It's snowing!" she said, giggling.

A marshmallow landed in my hair. I picked it out and ate it. "Mmmmmm. Yummy!" I said, and smiled at Kasey.

"Freddy, please pick up those marshmallows," said my mom.

I got down on the floor, picked up a marshmallow, and popped it into my mouth.

"Freddy, what are you doing?" said my mom. "You don't eat food off the floor! You're not a dog!"

Kelly and Kasey patted my head. I barked and pretended to wag my tail.

"All right. Enough silliness for one night,"

said my mom. "Let's clean this mess and drink up. We've got a busy day tomorrow."

"What are we going to do?" Kasey asked.

"We are going to the tree farm to cut down our own Christmas tree!" I said, doing a little dance.

"Ooh. We've never done that before," said the twins. "We can't wait!"

"It's so much fun!" said Suzie. "You're going to love it!"

CHAPTER 4

Wake Up, Rudolph!

The next morning Kelly, Kasey, and I decided to wake up Suzie by playing "Rudolph the Red-Nosed Reindeer" on kazoos they had brought.

"Doo-doo, doo-doo, dooo, dooo, dooo," we buzzed as we marched around Suzie's sleeping bag.

Suzie jumped up. "What's going on?" she said.

Kelly, Kasey, and I were all giggling.

"What's so funny?" she asked.

"Nothing." We giggled some more.

"You guys are up to something," she said. "I'll be right back. I just have to go to the bathroom."

She ran into the bathroom, and as she passed the mirror, she stopped and did a double take. The word *Rudolph* was written in red lipstick on her forehead, and Kasey had colored her nose red.

The girls went running into the bathroom, laughing. "We did it while you were sleeping," said Kasey.

"Isn't it hilarious?" asked Kelly.

"Hey, Rudolph," I said, "where's Santa?"

"Ha-ha. Very funny," Suzie said. "I can't go to the tree farm like this. I look like a weirdo. Besides, Freddy, you know Mom will kill us if she finds out you used her good red lipstick."

"She doesn't have to know," I said.

"What's it worth to you?" asked Suzie, holding up her pinkie for a pinkie swear.

"How about two pieces of candy from my stocking?" I said.

"Two pieces? Is that all?" said Suzie. "You used Mom's *favorite* lipstick."

"Three pieces?"

"It's five or nothing," said Suzie, pushing her pinkie into my face. "Is it a deal?"

"Oh, all right, deal," I said, locking pinkies

with Suzie. I didn't really have a choice. It had been Kelly and Kasey's idea, but my mom was never going to believe that! And it was worth it, because Suzie looked hilarious!

Suzie washed her face. Then we all got dressed and headed down to breakfast.

"Good morning, everyone," said my mom. "How did you girls sleep?"

"I slept great, Aunt Debbie," said Kelly.

"Me, too," said Kasey.

My mom walked over to Suzie and stared at her. "Suzie, you have a red mark on your nose."

I gulped. Kelly, Kasey, and I looked at one another. Then I mouthed to Suzie, "We have a deal."

"Oh, it's probably just red marker. We were all making Christmas cards this morning. I might have had some marker on my hand and then scratched my nose."

"Are you sure that's all it is?"

"I'm fine, Mom, really," Suzie said.

"Well, okay. Come have some breakfast."

We each breathed a sigh of relief.

"Eat up, everybody," said my dad. "We've got to get going."

"Yeah, we have to get to the tree farm before all the best trees are gone!" I said.

"Oh, there are plenty of nice trees to choose from," said my mom.

"I don't want a nice tree. I want the *perfect* tree!"

"Don't worry, Freddy. We'll help you find the perfect tree," said the twins.

"How about Papa and Grammy?" asked Suzie. "Are they coming?"

"They were a little tired from the trip," said my mom. "They decided to sleep in for a while this morning. We'll see them when we get back."

"Then let's get a move on," said my dad.

"Does everyone have their winter coat?" asked Mom.

"Yes!" we all said.

"You also need a hat and mittens," said my mom. "It's always cold at the tree farm."

"Got them right here!" I said, pointing to my favorite shark hat and mittens. The mittens looked like shark heads with teeth.

"These sharks are going to take a big bite out of that tree!" I said, chomping at the air with my hands.

Suzie looked at me and made a "cuckoo" sign with her finger.

My cousins laughed. "All right, Shark Boy. Let's go."

We all hopped in the car.

"This is so cool," said Kelly.

"I can't wait," said Kasey. "I've never cut down my own Christmas tree before!"

"It's a blast!" said Suzie.

When we got to White's Tree Farm, Suzie, the twins, and I jumped out of the car and started running toward the rows of trees.

"Wait!" my dad called. "Come back!"

"Why?" I asked.

"We have to go get the saw from that man over there."

We ran over to the guy handing out the saws. "One saw, please," I said.

"I have to give the saw to an adult. This is not a toy. Is your mom or dad here?" the man said.

Just then my dad came running up. "I'm right here. I'll be in charge of that," he said, taking the saw from the man. "Thanks so much."

"Don't forget your sled," said the man.

"A sled! A sled!" said Kasey and Kelly. "You didn't tell us that we were going sledding!"

"The sled isn't for you," the man said, laughing. "It's for the tree."

"Why would the tree need a sled?" asked Kasey.

"Trees don't go sledding," said Kelly. "That would be pretty funny to see a Christmas tree riding down a hill on a sled. Whee!"

"No, no, no," said the man. "After you chop down the tree, you put it on the sled and drag it back to your car. It's much easier than carrying it back."

"Oh, I get it," said Kelly.

"Good idea!" said Kasey.

"Jump on, Freddy," said the twins. "Since we don't have a tree right now, we'll give *you* a ride."

I jumped onto the sled. They grabbed the rope handle and took off running.

CHAPTER 5

The Perfect Tree

The twins were pulling me so fast that it felt like I was flying.

I stuck my arms out to the sides. "It's a car. It's a train. It's Su-per-man!"

Then we hit a bump, and I went sailing off the sled and landed face-first in the snow.

My mom, my dad, and Suzie ran over. "Freddy, are you all right?" they asked.

I slowly lifted my head and spit out some

snow that had gotten in my mouth. “I think so,” I said.

“That was awesome,” said Kelly.

“Yeah, that looked like a trick from the X Games,” said Kasey.

I stood up slowly.

"You already broke your arm once, Freddy," said my mom. "I really don't want to spend Christmas in the emergency room, so let's just use the sled for the tree."

"Okeydokey, Aunt Debbie," said Kelly.

"No more sled rides," said Kasey.

We left the sled with my mom and started running through the rows of trees.

I ran along a few rows, and then, all of a sudden, I stopped in my tracks. There it was . . . right in front of me . . . the most perfect tree I had ever seen.

I jumped up and down and waved my hands in the air. "Hey, over here! Over here!" I shouted. "I found it! I found it!"

Kelly, Kasey, and Suzie ran over.

"You look like you have ants in your pants," said Kasey.

"Why are you doing a crazy dance in the middle of the tree farm?" asked Kelly.

"You are such a goofball," said Suzie.

"I found it!" I said again.

"Found what?" asked my mom and dad, who had finally caught up to us.

"The perfect tree," I said, pointing to my right. "Just look at it. There are no broken branches. It's perfectly round, and it's just the right size. Not too big . . . not too small. Like I said, it's perfect."

"Sounds like you want it to be your girlfriend," said Kelly.

"Or maybe since you love it so much, you should marry it," said Kasey.

Suzie burst out laughing. "Freddy should marry the tree! That's a good one, Kasey."

"It *is* a pretty tree," said my mom.

"Can we chop it down?" I asked.

"Chop it! Chop it!" the twins chanted as they karate chopped the air.

"Do we all agree that this is the tree we want?" asked my dad.

We all nodded.

"Then here we go."

My dad bent down and started sawing the trunk of the tree.

"Hey, look, I'm a tree," said Kasey, standing perfectly still. "Freddy, pretend you're chopping me down."

I ran over and pretended to saw her legs.

"Timber!" she yelled, and fell over in the snow.

"Ha, ha, ha. That looks fun!" said Kelly. "Chop me down, Freddy."

I pretended to saw her legs, and she fell over, too.

"My turn," I said.

Kasey chopped me, and I toppled over.

"Watch out!" yelled my dad. "Here comes the real thing."

"Timber!" we all shouted, and the tree hit the ground with a *thud*.

"Let's load it onto the sled," said my dad.

"Come on, everybody," said my mom. "Grab a piece of the tree. One, two, three, lift!"

We all picked up the tree and put it on the sled.

"Come on, little tree. Time for a ride," Kelly said.

The twins pulled the sled, and Suzie and I pushed from the back.

"Great teamwork, everyone," said my dad

when we got to the car. "I just have to tie it to the roof."

We returned the sled and the saw and paid for the tree. The man gave us each a candy cane. "Merry Christmas!" he said.

"Merry Christmas!" we yelled out the car window.

"Can I borrow your candy cane for a minute?" Kelly asked her sister.

Kasey handed it to her.

Kelly stuck the ends of hers and Kasey's into her mouth. "Look at me. I'm a walrus!" she said.

Suzie and I laughed.

"Eeewww, now it's got your cooties all over it," said Kasey. "Give it back." Her sister handed it back, and Kasey held it up to her forehead. "Now look at me. I'm a unicorn."

"I have an idea," said Suzie. "Freddy, give me yours for a minute."

I gave mine to Suzie, and she held it and

hers on top of her head. "Guess who I am," she said.

We stared at her for a minute.

"I'll give you a hint," said Suzie. She patted her nose.

"Rudolph the Red-Nosed Reindeer!" we all said.

"Had a very shiny nose," my mom sang.

We all looked at each other and burst out laughing.

"What's so funny?" asked my mom.

"Oh, nothing. Nothing," we said, and giggled some more.

When we got home, Papa and Grammy were waiting for us.

"I found the perfect tree!" I shouted. "Wait until you see it!"

My dad untied the tree from the roof of the car, and we all helped him carry it into the house.

"Great job, kids!" said my dad. "We just have to get it in the tree stand over there."

We set the tree in the tree stand and stood back. "Now that is a beautiful tree," said Papa.

"It looks perfect to me, Freddy," said Grammy.

Slowly, the tree started to lean to one side, and then it started falling toward the coffee table at full speed.

I ran over and caught it just in time before it hit the table.

"Wow! Great catch, Freddy," said Papa.

"That would have been a real disaster," said Grammy.

"You saved the day!" said Kelly.

"Superman to the rescue!" said Kasey.

I held up both my arms to show my muscles.

Suzie rolled her eyes. "Oh, puh-leez," she said.

We put the tree back in the stand and tightened it.

"That should hold now," said my dad.

"Sit, little tree . . . stay . . . ," said Kasey, pointing to it.

"What are you doing?" I asked.

"Getting the tree to stay."

"But the tree isn't a dog."

"I know, but it works on our dogs, Mike and Ike, so I thought it might work on the tree, too," Kasey said.

We all looked at her and started laughing.

"Come on, all of you crazy kids," said my mom. "Time for lunch!"

CHAPTER 6

What's That Smell?

After lunch, it was time to make gingerbread cookies.

"I love gingerbread cookies," said Kasey, licking her lips.

"They're *my* favorite, too!" I said. "And wait until you taste them. They are the best gingerbread cookies in the world!"

My mom and Grammy laughed.

"That's because they are made from Grammy's secret recipe," said my mom.

"What makes them so yummy?" I asked.

"If I told you, then it wouldn't be a secret, now, would it?" Grammy said, smiling.

"But it is a family tradition to make Grammy's gingerbread cookies every Christmas," said my mom. "We're so glad you girls are here this year to make them with us."

"We eat a bunch, and we leave some for Santa," I said.

"I made the dough while you were at the tree farm this morning," said Grammy. "All you have to do is roll it out, cut it with cookie cutters, and decorate."

"I love to use the rolling pin. Can I help you roll it out, Grammy?" asked Kelly.

"Sure. Let me just put some flour down on the counter so the dough doesn't stick."

Grammy sprinkled some flour on the counter, and Kelly started to roll out the dough.

My mom turned the oven on so it could heat up.

Quietly, Kasey grabbed the flour sack and stuck her hand inside.

"What are you doing?" I whispered.

"Just watch," she whispered back.

She took a handful of flour and sprinkled it in her hair. Then, in a voice that sounded just like Grammy's, she said, "I hope you like my secret recipe."

My mom turned around, and her mouth fell open. She is a neat freak, and my cousin had flour in her hair, and it was sprinkled all over the floor by her feet.

I was trying not to laugh.

My mom ran over to the table. "Kasey, what are you doing?" she said.

"I'm Grammy Rose. See my gray hair?" Kasey said, pointing to the flour in her hair.

"I see," said my mom, trying to stay calm. "Why don't you come over to the sink, and we'll shake that flour out of your hair. Suzie, would you please grab the broom and sweep up all the flour on the floor?"

We got everything cleaned up while Grammy helped Kelly finish rolling out the dough. "All righty," said Grammy, "the dough is all ready." She gave each of us a piece.

Kelly grabbed a reindeer cookie cutter. "I think I'll make Rudolph," she said, smiling.

"I'll stick one of these red candies on the end of his nose. What do you think?"

I giggled. "I think it looks just like Suzie," I whispered.

"I'm going to make a pair of twin gingerbread girl cookies," said Suzie. "Just like Kelly and Kasey."

"That's a cute idea," said Grammy.

Grammy turned to Kasey. "And what are you making, sweetie? A girl? A boy? Santa?"

Kasey laughed. "Nope. I'm making a gingerbread alien!"

"A gingerbread alien!" I said. "That's so cool!"

"See?" said Kasey. "It's got two antennae, and I made three eyes out of green gumdrops."

"It looks just like one of the aliens from the *Commander Upchuck* episode I watched last week."

"I watch that show every week, too! That's where I got the idea," said Kasey.

My mom started sniffing the air. *Sniff. Sniff. Sniff.* "I smell something funny," she said.

"I smell it, too," said Grammy. "It smells kind of like burning rubber."

"I think it's coming from over here," my mom said as she walked toward the oven.

She opened the oven door and a huge cloud of black smoke poured out.

The fire alarm started to go off. *BEEP! BEEP! BEEP!*

My dad ran into the kitchen. "What's going on in here?"

"I don't know!" said my mom. "Something's burning in the oven!"

"Maybe it's the cookies," said my dad.

"We haven't put any in yet."

My dad put on some oven mitts and ran over to the oven. He fanned the smoke out of the way so he could see inside.

Then he reached in and carefully pulled something out.

"What is it?" asked my mom.

"Boots," said my dad.

"Boots?"

"Yep. Snow boots."

"What in the world . . . ?" said Grammy.

"Oops," Kelly whispered.

We all turned and looked at her.

"Kelly, do these belong to you?" asked my dad.

She nodded.

"What were they doing in the oven?" asked my mom.

"I'm so sorry, Aunt Debbie. When we got home from the tree farm, my boots were soaked. I thought if I put them in the oven, they might dry quicker. But I forgot all about them!"

I thought my mom was going to explode. I could tell that my wacky cousins were driving her a little crazy!

"I'm really, really sorry, Aunt Debbie."

My mom took a few deep breaths. “Things are always exciting with you two around,” she said to my cousins. “Let me just clean out the oven, and then we can bake the cookies.”

“Good idea, Mom!” I said. “We need to leave a plate of cookies for Santa. Not a plate of boots!”

CHAPTER 7

Reindeer Food

"Hey, why don't we decorate the Christmas tree while the cookies are baking?" I said.

"Great idea, Freddy!" said the twins.

We ran into the living room.

"I'm going to turn on some Christmas music," said Suzie. "I love listening to Christmas songs when we trim the tree."

"Where are the ornaments?" asked Kasey.

"They are all right here in this big box," I said. "Help yourself."

"You can hang them anywhere you want," said Suzie.

"Look at this one," said Kelly. "It looks like a snowman made out of marshmallows!"

"Maybe it's Frosty the Snowman," I said.

Just then the Frosty song started playing, and we all started singing, "Frosty the Snowman was a jolly, happy soul . . ."

Kasey grabbed three round ornaments out of the box and started to juggle them.

I giggled. "You look like one of the clowns in the circus!" I said. "Where did you learn to do that?"

"My dad taught me," she said.

"Maybe sometime when I come to visit he can teach me," I said.

"Sure!" said Kasey. "And I can show you my marshmallow shooter."

"No way! You have one of those? I've always wanted one!"

Kelly picked up another ornament. It was a frame with a picture of me as a baby. "Oh, look how cute little Freddy Spaghetti was when he was an itty-bitty baby."

"He was a little baldy," said Kasey. "With just a little fuzz on top."

"And look at those chubby cheeks," said Grammy. "You were so adorable."

"Now look at you," said Suzie, laughing. "What happened?"

I glared at her.

"I think Freddy is just as adorable today as he was when he was a baby," said Grammy. And she gave me a big kiss on the cheek.

"Thanks, Grammy," I said.

We put some more ornaments on the tree, and then my mom walked into the room.

"Where's the star?" she asked.

"Right here!" said Kelly, pointing to herself. She started to do a little tap dance.

"I meant the star that goes on top of the tree," my mom said, laughing.

"It's right here," said Suzie. "I was just unwrapping it."

"Be very careful," said my mom. "I don't want it to break."

"Can I put it on this year?" I asked. "Pretty please with a cherry on top?"

"That's not fair," said Suzie. "I want to."

"Well, I asked first."

"But I'm the one holding it," said Suzie.

"Freddy, Suzie, no fighting," said my dad.

"I have an idea," said my mom. "How about we have one of our guests do it?"

"Good idea," said my dad.

"Kelly, Kasey—Wait a minute. Where is Kasey?"

"Has anyone seen Kasey?" asked my dad.

We looked around. She wasn't in the room.

"Where could she be?" said Grammy.

"I'll go look for her," said my mom.

"We'll come, too!" we all said.

"I bet she went upstairs to get something from your room, Suzie," my mom said. "Let's check there first."

We walked down the hall and started up the stairs. Something crunched under our feet.

"I think I just stepped on something," said Suzie.

"Me, too," I said.

My mom bent down and picked something up off the carpet.

"What is it?" I asked.

My mom smelled it. "I think it's granola," she said.

"Granola? Why would there be granola on the stairs?"

"I'm wondering the same thing myself."

There was a trail of granola that went all the way up the stairs and into Suzie's bedroom.

When we got to the bedroom, we found Kasey sprinkling the rest of the box all over Suzie's room.

"Hi, everybody!" Kasey said.

"Oh boy," I thought. "This is not going to be good." My mom never lets us bring food up to our rooms. She thinks it will leave crumbs, and then we will get ants. She hates ants!

My mom just stood there with her mouth hanging open. She couldn't talk. Nothing came out.

Finally, she started to speak. "Wh-wh-what are you doing, Kasey?" she asked.

"I'm leaving food for the reindeer."

"For the what?" said my mom.

"For Santa's reindeer. Every year we put granola on the front lawn so that the reindeer can have a little snack. But I never get to see them when they are outside. I thought if I sprinkled some in the house, they might follow the trail right up to Suzie's room, and then I might get to see Rudolph!"

My mom shook her head.

"Where do you girls come up with these ideas?"

"Our own heads," they said together.

"You two are quite a pair," she said. "Quite a pair . . ."

CHAPTER 8

Christmas Morning

When I woke up on Christmas morning, I looked in my cousins' sleeping bags, but they weren't there.

"Hey, Suzie," I said. "Where are Kelly and Kasey?"

"In their sleeping bags," she said.

"No, they're not."

Suzie sat up in bed. "What do you mean?"

"I mean they're not there. See for yourself."

Suzie got up and walked over to their sleeping bags. "Where could they be?"

"Shhhh," I said. "I think I hear a noise coming from downstairs."

Suzie and I raced downstairs to the living room. There were Kelly and Kasey, asleep behind the Christmas tree, snoring like two grizzly bears in winter.

I shook them to wake them up. "What are you guys doing down here?" I asked.

They rubbed their eyes.

"We came downstairs last night because we wanted to see Santa," said Kelly.

"But we didn't want him to see us, so we hid behind the Christmas tree," said Kasey.

"Did you see him?" I asked. "Does he really have a big white beard, and does his belly jiggle like a bowlful of jelly when he laughs?"

The twins frowned. "We must have fallen asleep before he came," said Kelly.

"We didn't get to see him," said Kasey. "Bummer!"

"We can try again next year," said Kelly.

"Good idea, sis," said Kasey.

Just then my parents and Papa and Grammy came downstairs.

"Merry Christmas, kids," said Papa.

"Merry Christmas, Papa," we all said.

"You kids are up bright and early," said Grammy.

"It's Christmas morning," I said. "Kids always get up early on Christmas morning!"

"It looks like Santa was here," said my dad. "There isn't even enough room under the tree for all the presents!"

"Can we open our presents? Can we, Dad? Can we?" I said.

"Pre-sents! Pre-sents!" the twins chanted.

"Let me just get the video camera ready, and then you can start unwrapping."

"Can we open Kelly's and Kasey's presents first?" I asked.

"Sure," said my mom.

"I'm all set," said my dad. "Go for it."

"Here, Freddy, this one is from us," said the twins, handing me a gift.

I ripped open the paper. "Yes!" I exclaimed. "An ant farm! I've always wanted one of these."

"Did you say 'ant farm'?" asked my mom.

"Yep, with real, live ants!"

"Fabulous," my mom said, shaking her head.

"Here, Suzie, we picked this one out just for you," said the twins.

Suzie unwrapped the package. "Ooh, a Sassy doll. I love these!" she said. "Thanks, you guys."

"It's the fashion one," said Kelly. "You can change the outfits."

"You can also do the hair and makeup," said Kasey.

"Those are very thoughtful gifts," said Grammy.

"Now it's your turn," I said to the twins, handing them each a package.

"We hope you like them!" said Suzie.

The girls unwrapped their packages at the same time.

"Wow! A baton!" said Kasey.

"With rainbow sparkles!" said Kelly.

"We're taking a new dance class, and we're learning how to do baton," said Kasey.

"Do you want to see?" asked Kelly.

Before my mom could say no, Kasey and Kelly threw their batons up in the air.

Kelly caught hers, but Kasey's baton sailed over our heads and flew toward the Christmas tree.

"Oh no!" my mom yelled.

The baton hit the top branch and knocked the star off the tree.

My mom covered her eyes.

"I got it! I got it!" I yelled. I made a diving catch before the star hit the ground.

"Wow, Freddy! That was some catch!" said Papa. "You should be an outfielder."

"And I caught it all on camera," my dad said, smiling.

"Well, this has been a very crazy Christmas!" my mom said.

"You can say that again," I said, laughing.

"You girls are definitely one of a kind," my mom said.

Kelly and Kasey put their arms around each other. "Actually, we're two of a kind," they said.

"Merry Christmas, everyone!" said Papa. "Merry Christmas!"

DEAR READER,

I just love the holidays! We spend Christmas with grandparents and cousins, just like Freddy's family. Our family has some special holiday traditions, too.

We go to White's Tree Farm and cut down our own Christmas tree. When we bring it home, it makes the whole house smell like Christmas.

We make homemade gingerbread cookies and decorate them. We usually end up eating most of them on Christmas Eve, but we always save a few to leave for Santa!

We sprinkle granola on the front lawn for Santa's reindeer. They must get hungry doing all that flying!

I hope you have as much fun reading *A Very Crazy Christmas* as I had writing it.

HAPPY HOLIDAYS AND HAPPY READING!

Abby Klein

Freddy's Fun Pages

FREDDY'S SHARK JOURNAL

ALL ABOUT RAYS

Rays are cousins of sharks, like Kelly and Kasey are Freddy's cousins. Here are some things you might not know about rays.

- Both sharks and rays have skeletons made of cartilage.
- Rays glide through the water by beating their winglike fins.
- A ray's mouth and gill slits are on the underside of its body.
- Many types of rays have eyes on top of their heads to see predators swimming above them.

One manta ray had a wingspan that was as wide as four cars!

Stingrays have poisonous stingers on their tails. Beware!

GRAMMY ROSE'S "SECRET" GINGERBREAD COOKIE RECIPE

Would you like to make gingerbread cookies and decorate them, like Freddy and his cousins did? Grammy's recipe makes the best cookies in the world! Shhhhh...just don't tell her we shared her secret with you!

In a small bowl, whisk:

3 cups all-purpose flour
1 ½ teaspoons baking powder
¾ teaspoon baking soda
¼ teaspoon salt
1 tablespoon ground ginger
1 ¾ teaspoons ground cinnamon
¼ teaspoon ground cloves

Put these dry ingredients aside.

Ask an adult to help you beat in a separate bowl until blended:

6 tablespoons unsalted butter
¾ cup dark brown sugar
1 large egg

When it is blended, add:

½ cup molasses
2 teaspoons vanilla

Then gradually add the dry ingredients from your small bowl until everything is blended and smooth.

Divide the dough in half and wrap each half in plastic wrap. Let it stand at room temperature for AT LEAST 2 hours.

Ask an adult to preheat the oven to 375 degrees and help you grease your cookie sheets.

Place some of the dough on a floured surface to roll it out. Before you start, sprinkle some flour over the dough and on the rolling pin.

Roll out the dough until it is about ¼-inch thick.

Cut out your cookies with your favorite cookie cutters and place them on a cookie sheet about an inch apart.

Ask an adult to put the cookie sheet in the oven. Bake for 7 to 10 minutes—less time if you want softer cookies, and more time if you prefer them crunchy.

When they are done, have an adult help you take them out of the oven, and let them cool.

Once they are cool, you can frost them and decorate them any way you like.

Eat and enjoy!

PINECONE CHRISTMAS TREE

Make your own mini Christmas tree using a pinecone!

YOU WILL NEED:

a dry pinecone
green glitter
glue and scissors
sequins and/or tinsel
yellow paper
a paintbrush

DIRECTIONS:

1. Paint the pinecone with glue.

2. Before the glue dries, sprinkle it with green glitter.

3. When it dries, glue on sequins or tinsel.

4. Cut a small star out of the yellow paper and glue it on top.

Use your mini tree as a Christmas decoration in your house!

CRAZY CHRISTMAS JOKES

Here are some of Kelly and Kasey's favorite Christmas jokes. Try them on your friends!

1. What do elves learn in school?
   The elf-abet

2. What does Santa do in his garden?
   Hoe, hoe, hoe!

3. What does Frosty the Snowman eat for breakfast?
   Frosted flakes

4. What is red, white, and blue at Christmas?
   A sad candy cane (or a candy cane without any presents!)

5. Knock knock.
   Who's there?
   Mary.
   Mary who?
   Mary Christmas!

Have you read all about Freddy?

Don't miss any of Freddy's funny adventures!

These twins are Double the Trouble!